Library of Congress Cataloging-in-Publication Data Available

10 9 8 7 6 5 4 3 2 1

Published by Sterling Publishing Co., Inc.
387 Park Avenue South, New York, NY 10016
Originally published in 1995 by Tambourine Books
Text copyright © 2004 by Harriet Ziefert
Illustrations copyright © by Emily Bolam
Distributed in Canada by Sterling Publishing
c/o Canadian Manda Group, One Atlantic Avenue, Suite 105
Toronto, Ontario, Canada M6K 3E7
Distributed in Great Britain and Europe by Chris Lloyd at Orca Book
Services, Stanley House, Fleets Lane, Poole BH15 3AJ, England
Distributed in Australia by Capricorn Link (Australia) Pty. Ltd.
P.O. Box 704, Windsor, NSW 2756, Australia

Printed in China
All rights reserved

Sterling ISBN: 1-4027-1704-0

OH, WHAT A NOISY FARM!

by Harriet Ziefert
Pictures by Emily Bolam

Sterling Publishing Co., Inc.
New York

Because the bull was chasing the cow,
the farmer's wife shouted...

STOP, STOP, YOU BIG OLD BULL!

and chased them around the pasture.

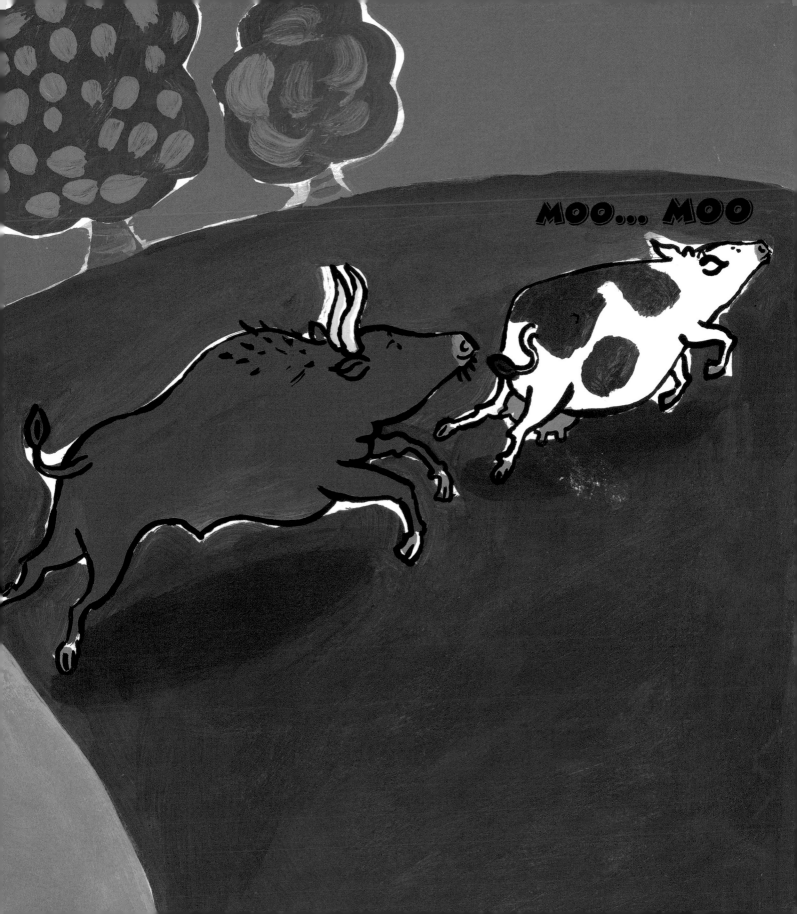

The farmer heard:
STOP, STOP...MOO, MOO!
and ran after the cow,
the bull, and his wife.

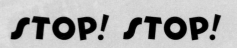

The goat heard:

STOP, STOP...MOO, MOO...

and ran after the cow, the bull,

the farmer, and his wife.

BLEAT...

BLEAT!

STOP!

The goose heard:

STOP, STOP...MOO, MOO...

BLEAT, BLEAT...and ran after the goat,

the cow, the bull, the farmer, and his wife.

STOP!

HONK!

The dog heard:

STOP, STOP...MOO, MOO...

BLEAT, BLEAT...HONK, HONK...

and ran after the goose, the goat, the cow,

the bull, the farmer, and his wife.

The cat heard:

STOP, STOP...MOO, MOO...

BLEAT, BLEAT...HONK, HONK...

BOW WOW, BOW WOW...

and ran after the dog, the goose, the goat,

the cow, the bull, the farmer, and his wife.

With the farmer's wife **SHOUTING**,
the cow **MOO MOOING**,
the goat **BLEAT BLEATING**,

HONK! HONK!

MEOW...
MEOW

the goose **HONK HONKING**,
the dog **BOW WOWING**,
and the cat **MEOWING**—

EVERYONE WAS TOO TIRED
TO MAKE ANY MORE NOISE.